Meagan &
Enjoy a li
happy family
Gwen
xo

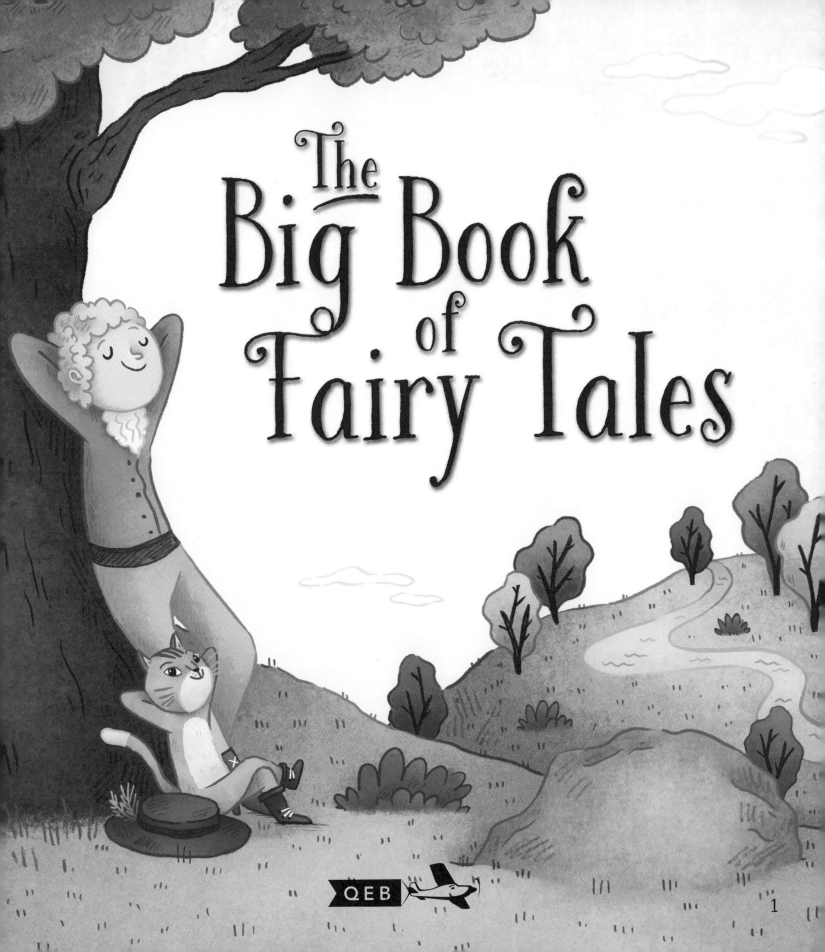

The Big Book of Fairy Tales

CONTENTS

Quarto is the authority on a wide range of topics.
Quarto educates, entertains and enriches the lives of our readers—enthusiasts and lovers of hands-on living.
www.quartoknows.com

Published in the United States by
QEB Publishing, Inc.
Part of The Quarto Group
6 Orchard Road
Lake Forest, CA 92630

A catalogue record for this book is available from the British Library.

ISBN 978 1 68297 328 8

Printed in China

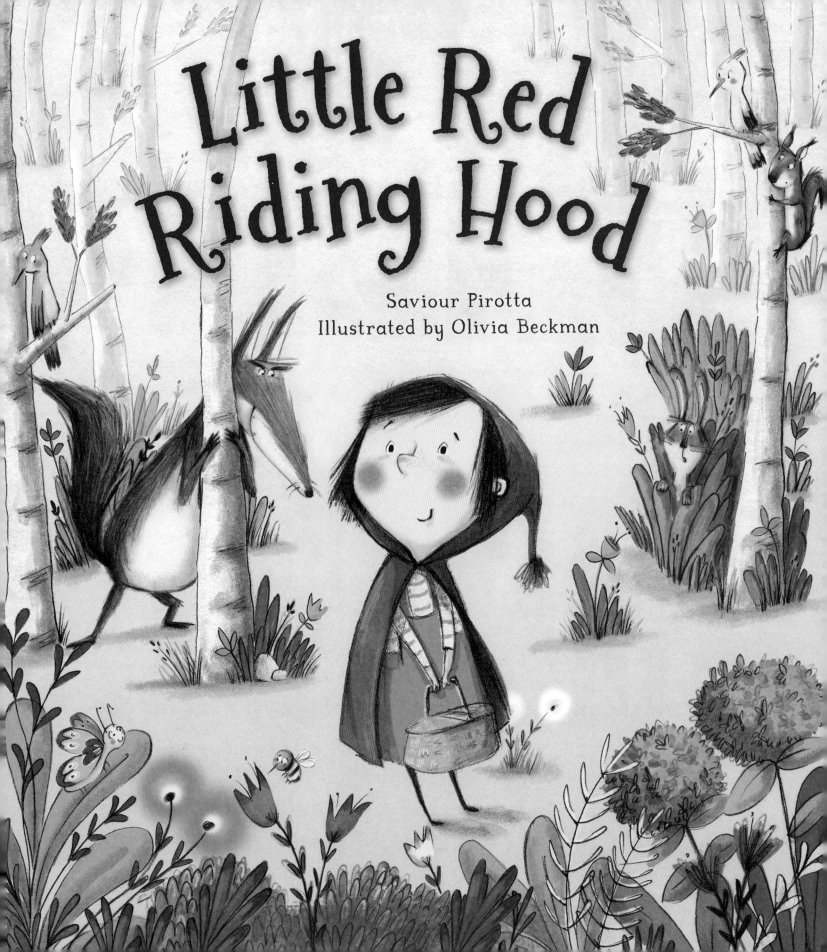

Little Red Riding Hood

Saviour Pirotta

Illustrated by Olivia Beckman

Once there was a girl
who had a lovely red coat,
with a red hood.

People called her **Little Red Riding Hood.**

One day her mother put some cakes in a basket. "Granny's ill," she said. "Why don't you go and see her?"

So Little Red Riding Hood
set off with the cakes.

"Stay on the path and
don't talk to strangers!"
warned her mother.

Little Red Riding Hood reached the woods and
saw some beautiful flowers. She wandered off
the path to pick some for her granny.

As soon as she left the
path, she met a wolf.

"What's in your basket?"
he asked sweetly.

"Cakes for my granny," answered
Little Red Riding Hood.

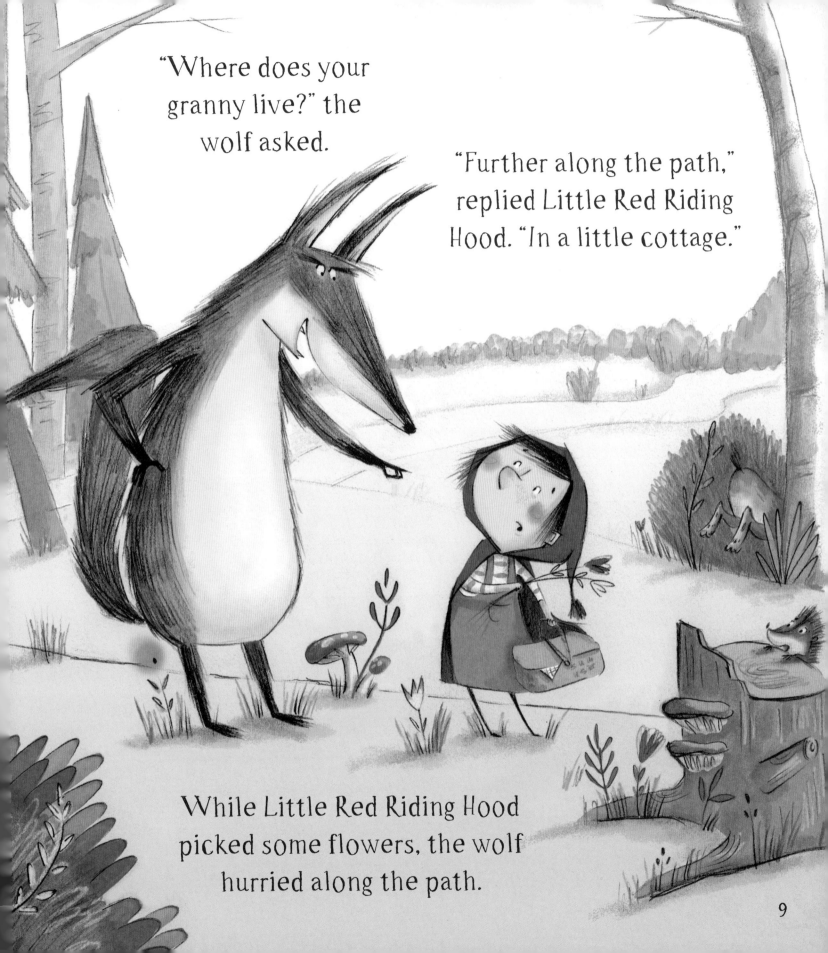

"Where does your granny live?" the wolf asked.

"Further along the path," replied Little Red Riding Hood. "In a little cottage."

While Little Red Riding Hood picked some flowers, the wolf hurried along the path.

When Little Red Riding Hood arrived
at Granny's cottage, she called out:

"Granny, it's me."

"Come in.
The door's open,"
wheezed Granny.

She was tucked up in bed,
with the curtains closed.

11

"Granny, what **big ears** you have!"
said Little Red Riding Hood.

"All the better to hear you with, my dear," Granny whispered.

"Granny, what **big eyes** you have!" said Little Red Riding Hood.

"All the better to see you with, my dear," said Granny.

"Granny, what **big teeth** you have!" said Little Red Riding Hood.

"All the better to **EAT** you with!" snarled Granny, leaping out of bed.

15

"Help!" Little Red Riding Hood cried.

It wasn't Granny at all. It was the big, bad wolf and he wanted to gobble her up!

16

The horrible wolf chased her around and around the cottage.

"Help! Help!"
Little Red Riding Hood shouted.

Luckily, a woodcutter
heard her calling and
ran to see what all
the noise was about.

18

The woodcutter saw the wolf and raised his ax.
The wolf took one look and jumped out the window.

"Thank you," said Little Red Riding Hood.
"You saved my life."

"You must never, ever talk to
wolves," said the woodcutter.
"What is that knocking?"

Little Red Riding Hood rushed over to open the wardrobe where the knocking was coming from. She found Granny, safe and well. The wolf had shut her inside.

"Goodness! Thank you," Granny said to Little Red Riding Hood and gave her a big hug.

Little Red Riding Hood put the kettle on
and they all had cake and a nice cup of cocoa.

And Little Red Riding Hood never strayed
off the path in the woods again.

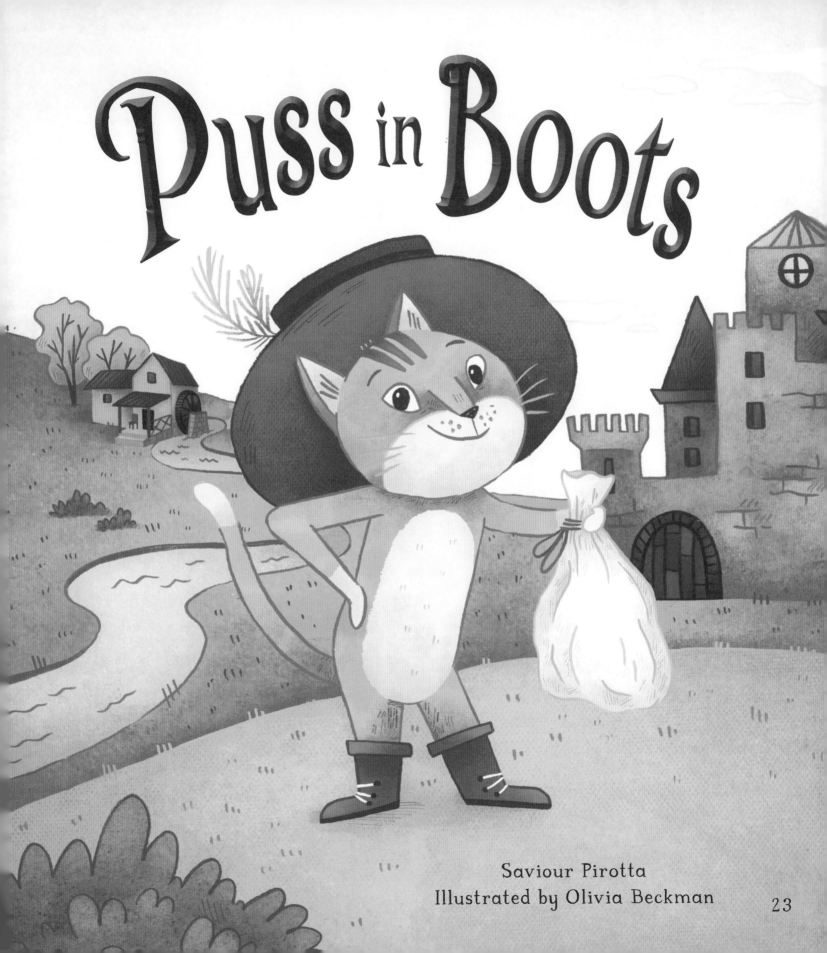

Puss in Boots

Saviour Pirotta
Illustrated by Olivia Beckman

Once there was a miller with three sons.

When the miller died, he left his eldest son his mill.

His second son his donkey.

And his youngest son, Bob...

...his **cat.**

"How will a cat help me earn a living?" sighed Bob.

"Give me a bag and a pair of boots," said the cat, "and I'll show you what my cunning and imagination can do."

Bob was so surprised to hear a
cat talk, that he did as he was asked.

27

The cat caught a wild rabbit with the bag.

He gave it to the king as a gift.

The next day he gave the king two partridges.

"Who is sending me these wonderful gifts?" asked the king.

"My master, the Lord of Carabas Castle," replied the cat.

The next morning, the cat took Bob to the river.
"Take off your clothes and swim in the river," he said.

"But it's freezing,"
complained Bob.

"Do as I say, and you'll soon be a prince," said the cat.
"When you see a carriage, pretend you are drowning."

Soon, the king and his
daughter drove past on
their early morning ride.

"Help!" shouted Bob.

"Thieves stole my
master's clothes and
threw him in the river,"
said the cat to the king.

31

The king ordered his men to rescue Bob and to fetch fine clothes to replace his stolen ones.

Bob looked like a prince in his new clothes. The king's daughter had never seen a finer looking man.

The king invited Bob to
join them on the ride.

Soon the carriage came
to a castle on a hill.

"That is Castle Carabas,"
said the cat. "Your Majesty
is welcome to visit, but allow
me to run ahead and make
everything ready."

The castle really belonged to a **horrible ogre.**

"I have heard," said the cat, "that you can change into anything you like."

"You heard right," chuckled the ogre.
And he turned into a roaring tiger.

"Ah," said the cat. "But I bet you can't change into something tiny, like a mouse?"

The ogre **roarrred** with laughter. "Can't I?"

38

The **roar** turned into a **squeak** as he changed into a mouse.

The cat pounced...
...and gobbled him up!

The king's carriage arrived
and the cat welcomed them
to Carabas Castle.

The princess was now
in love with Bob, and the king
was very impressed with the castle.

Bob and the princess were married soon after.

"Thank you, Puss," whispered Bob.
"Your cunning and imagination have
helped me to become a prince."

LORD PUSS IN BOOTS

The king was so happy, he made the cat a lord.
Everyone called him **Puss in Boots.**

44

THE GINGERBREAD MAN

Saviour Pirotta

Illustrated by Karl Newson

There was once a little old woman. She was hungry so she fetched some flour, butter, and sugar, and made a gingerbread man.

She gave him raisins for eyes and cherries for buttons.

When the gingerbread man was baked, the old woman
opened the oven. To her surprise, the gingerbread
man jumped out and ran through the door.

"STOP!"

shouted the old woman.
"I want you for my snack."

But the gingerbread man replied...

"Run, run, as fast as you can.
You'll never catch me.
I'm the gingerbread man."

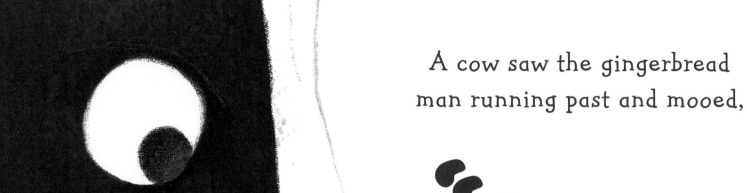

A cow saw the gingerbread man running past and mooed,

"STOP!

I want you for my lunch."

But the gingerbread man shouted,

"Run, run, as fast as you can.
You'll never catch me.
I'm the gingerbread man."

So the
old woman...

and the cow...

chased after the gingerbread man
but they couldn't catch him.

A pig saw the gingerbread man going by and grunted,

"STOP!

I want you for my supper."

But the gingerbread man sang,

"Run, run, as fast as you can.
You'll never catch me.
I'm the gingerbread man."

54

So the
old woman...

the cow...

and the pig...

chased after the gingerbread man,
but they still couldn't catch him.

Then the gingerbread man
came to a river.

"How will I ever get to the
other side?" he cried.

"Hop onto my tail,"
said a crafty fox.
"I'll carry you across."

57

The gingerbread man hopped onto the fox's tail.

The fox said, "You're getting wet there.
Why don't you sit on my back?"

So that's what the gingerbread man did.

Then the fox said,
"You're going to fall off
there. Why don't you
stand on my nose?"

So that's what the
gingerbread man did.

When they got to the other side, the fox flipped the gingerbread man up in the air with his nose and...

SNAP!

"**STOP!**"

cried the gingerbread man.
"That's half of me gone."

The fox flipped him
up a second time.

"**STOP!**"

cried the gingerbread man.
"That's almost all of me gone."

The fox flipped him up a third time and...

CRUUUUUNCH!

That was the end of the gingerbread man.

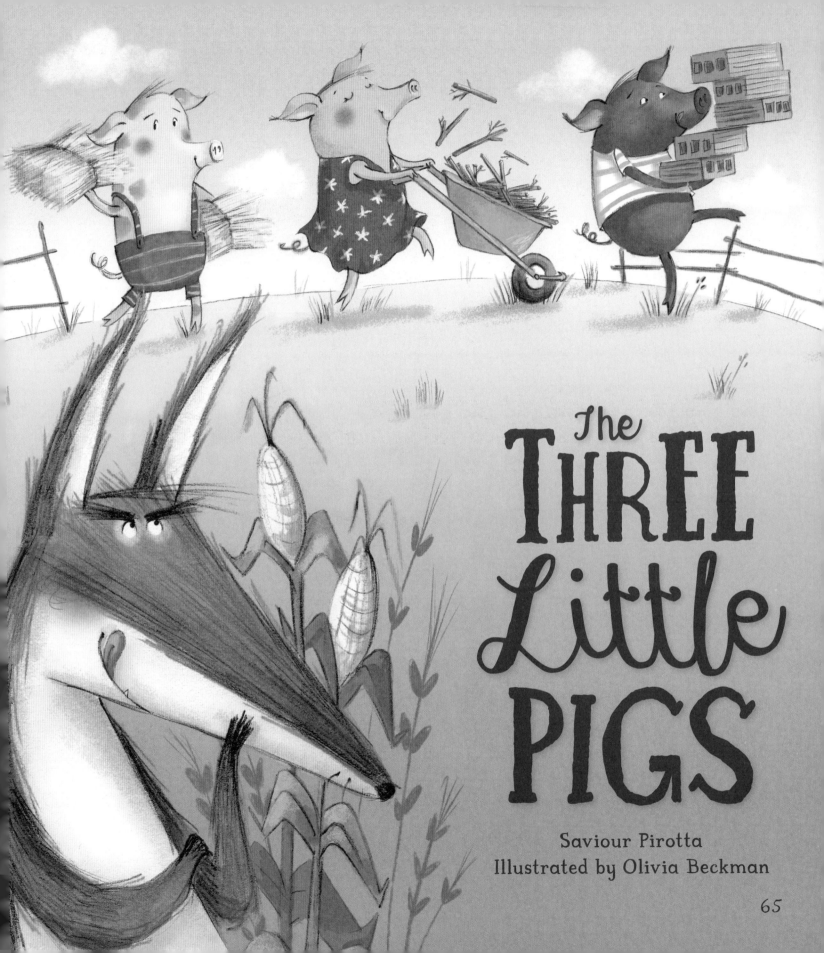

The THREE Little PIGS

Saviour Pirotta

Illustrated by Olivia Beckman

Three little pigs built themselves three little homes.

The first pig built a house with **straw.**

The second pig built
a house with **sticks.**

The third pig
built a house
with **bricks.**

No sooner had the first pig moved into
his house than the wolf came by.

He was very hungry and he could think of
nothing more tasty than a young juicy pig.

"Little pig, little pig, let me in."

The first pig replied,
"Not by the hair
on my chinny
chin chin."

"Then I'll **huff**, and I'll **puff**, and
I'll **blow** your house down,"
roared the wolf.

69

So he **huffed** and he **puffed** and he **blew** the straw house down.

The little pig ran away to his sister's house made of sticks.

Soon the wolf was at the door
of that house, too.

"Little pigs, little pigs, let me in."

The second pig squealed,
"Not by the hair on my
chinny chin chin."

"Then I'll **huff**, and I'll **puff**, and I'll **blow** your house down," howled the wolf.

So he **huffed** and he **puffed** and he **blew** the wooden house down.

74

The little pigs ran away to their brother's house made of bricks.

The wolf soon found that house, too.
He called, "Little pigs, little pigs, let me in."

The third pig replied,
"Not by the hair on my
chinny chin chin."

"Then I'll **huff,** and I'll **puff,** and
I'll **blow** your house down,"
shouted the wolf.

And he **huffed** and he **puffed** until he nearly **burst.**

But he could not blow the brick house down.

"Perhaps he'll go away?"
said the first pig.

"No," squealed the second pig. "I can see him climbing up the drainpipe."

"He'll try coming down the chimney," gasped the third pig.

79

The pigs cooked a pot of soup in the fireplace.

They removed the lid
and stoked up the fire.

81

The wolf sniggered. "I'm coming to eat you up, little pigs! One of you for breakfast, one for lunch, and one for dinner!"

But he jumped right
down the chimney...
straight into the
hot POT!

83

"Ouch," cried the wolf.

He hopped around the
house howling in pain.

The third pig threw
open the window and
the wolf leaped out.

The three little pigs knew he
would never bother them again.

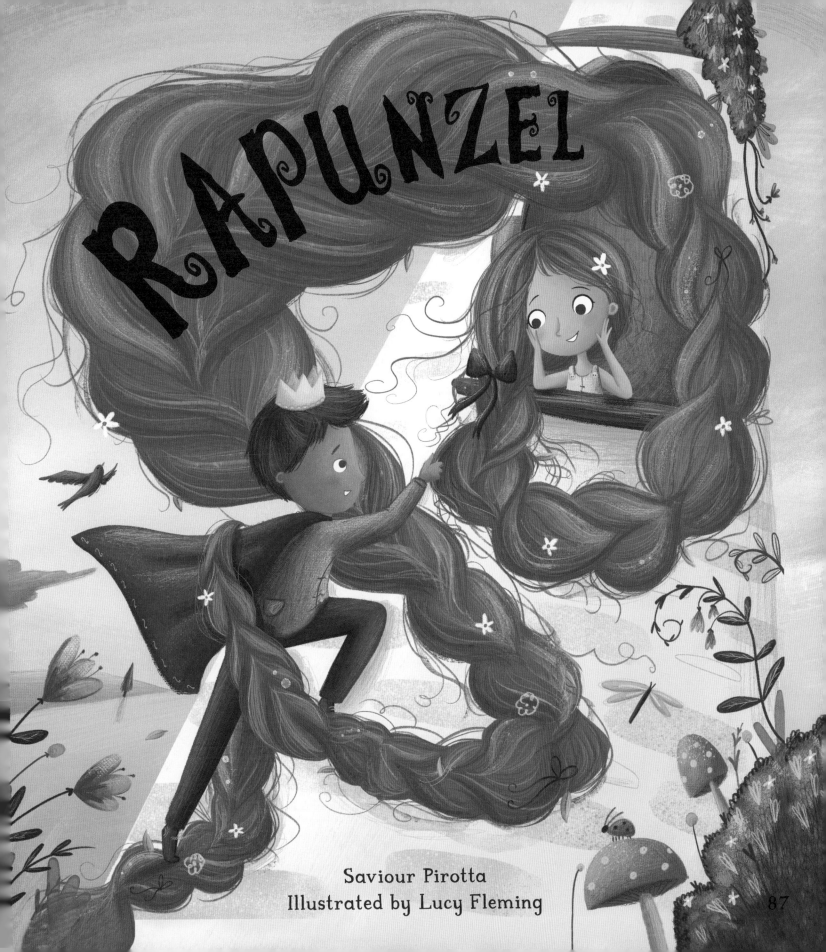

RAPUNZEL

Saviour Pirotta
Illustrated by Lucy Fleming

There was once a man and a
woman who lived next door to
a witch. The woman was pregnant
and she was always hungry.

A tasty herb, called rapunzel, grew in the witch's garden.
"I wish I could have some," sighed the woman.

The man didn't want his wife to be hungry so he sneaked
into the witch's garden and stole some rapunzel.

The woman wanted more rapunzel, so the man continued to steal it. Until one night, the witch caught him.

"Let me go," he begged.

"On one condition," cackled the witch.
"You must give me your newborn baby."

In his fear, the poor man
agreed and when the girl was
born, the witch carried her away.

91

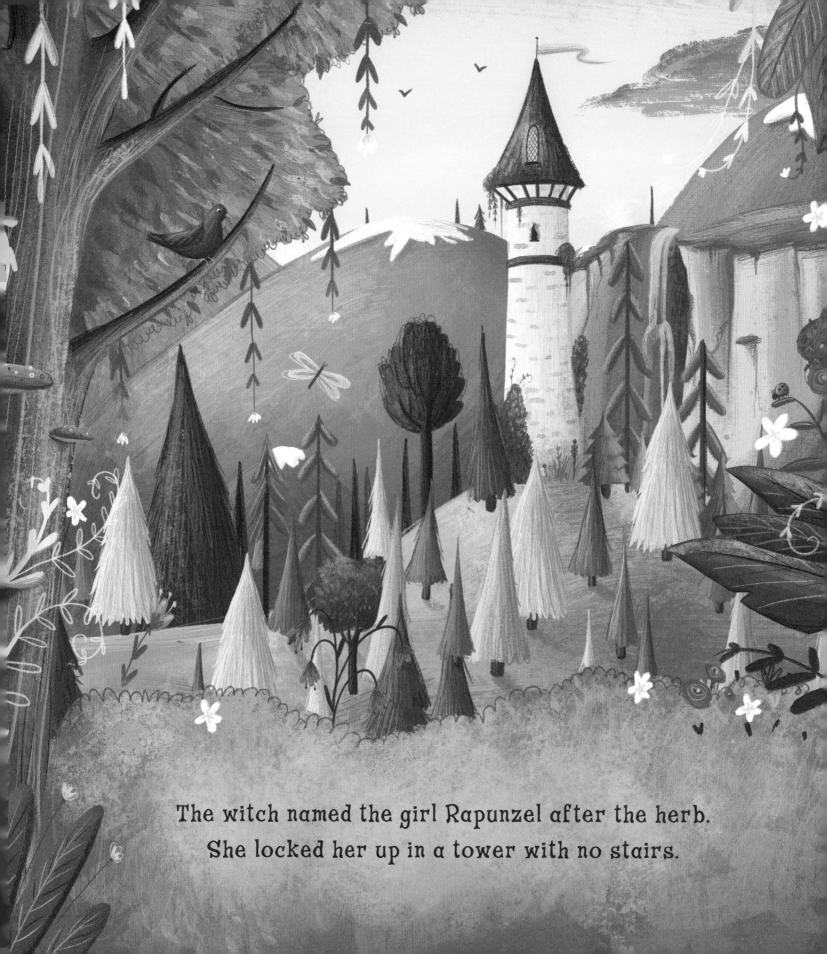

The witch named the girl Rapunzel after the herb.
She locked her up in a tower with no stairs.

As Rapunzel grew, so did her hair, in a long, flowing braid.

When the witch visited Rapunzel, she would call, "Rapunzel, Rapunzel, let down your hair."

Rapunzel would lean out of the window and the witch would climb up, using her braid like a rope.

93

Rapunzel was lonely and sad.
She would sit by the window
and look at far away towns
and villages, longing to go out.
She sang to pass the time.

Rapunzel didn't know that the
King's son often passed by the tower.
He was so enchanted by her voice
that he longed to meet her.

One day Rapunzel heard
a familiar cry. "Rapunzel,
Rapunzel, let down your hair."

But it was the prince, not the
witch, who climbed into the tower.

"I heard you sing and had to meet you," he said. "So I watched
from the bushes until I saw how the witch climbed up."

"You must go at once," cried Rapunzel, who had never seen such a beautiful face before. "If the witch finds you, she will hurt you."

"I shall return, my love," promised the prince. "And I shall help you escape."

Every night the prince returned with a handkerchief,
which Rapunzel used to make a rope. She hid it in
a chest, until one day the witch found it.

In an angry rage, she chopped off
Rapunzel's hair and cast a spell,
sending Rapunzel to the desert.

That night the prince arrived with another handkerchief.

"Rapunzel, Rapunzel, let down your hair," he cried.

Down came the hair, but it was the witch waiting for the prince in the tower.

She put a spell on him too, sending him into the forest.

For months, the prince wandered alone, singing to himself.

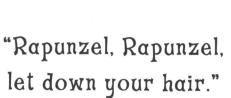

"Rapunzel, Rapunzel, let down your hair."

Until one day, finally, Rapunzel replied...

"Is that my prince?"

The prince and Rapunzel found each other at the point where the forest meets the desert.

105

Rapunzel and the prince were married
and they were never lonely again.

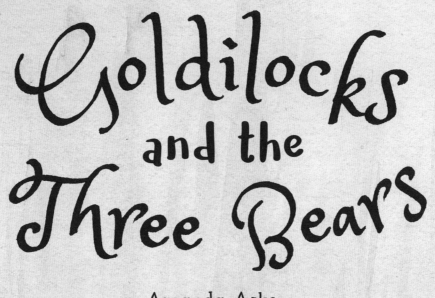

Goldilocks
and the
Three Bears

Amanda Askew
Illustrated by Bruno Merz

One day, a little girl called Goldilocks
went for a walk in the forest.

She came upon a house and knocked on the door. When no one answered, Goldilocks went inside.

At the table in the kitchen, there were three
bowls of porridge. Goldilocks was hungry.

She tasted the porridge
in the first bowl.

"This porridge is too hot!" she exclaimed.

Then she tasted the porridge
in the second bowl.

"This porridge is too cold!" she cried.

Finally, she tasted the last bowl of porridge.

"Ahh, this porridge is just right," she said.
And with that, she ate it all up.

After she'd eaten the porridge,
Goldilocks went into the living
room, where she saw three chairs.

She started to feel a little tired.

Goldilocks sat in the first chair to rest her feet.

"This chair is too hard!" she exclaimed.

Then she sat in the second chair.

"This chair is too big!" she whined.

Finally, she tried the last and smallest chair.

"Ahhh, this chair is just right," she sighed.

Just as she settled down into the
chair to rest, it broke into pieces.

Goldilocks wanted to lie down, so she decided to try the bedroom.

She lay down on the first bed, but it was too hard.

Then she lay down on the second bed, but it was too soft.

Last, she lay down on the
third bed, and it was just right.

Goldilocks fell asleep.

As she was sleeping, the three bears who lived in the cottage came home. They went into the kitchen, and what did they see?

"Someone's been eating my porridge," growled Papa Bear.

120

"Someone's been eating my porridge," said Mama Bear.

"Someone's been eating my porridge, and they've eaten it all up!" cried Baby Bear.

121

Next, the three bears went
into the living room, and
what did they see?

"Someone's been sitting in my chair," growled Papa Bear.

"Someone's been sitting in my chair," said Mama Bear.

"Someone's been sitting in my chair, and they've broken it to pieces," cried Baby Bear.

The three bears began to look around, and when they got to the bedroom, what did they see?

"Someone's been sleeping in my bed," growled Papa Bear.

"Someone's been sleeping in my bed," said Mama Bear.

"Someone's been sleeping in my bed, and she's still there!" cried Baby Bear.

125

Just then, Goldilocks woke up and saw the three bears.
The bears didn't look very happy.

"Help!" Goldilocks screamed.

She jumped up and ran out of the room.

Goldilocks ran out the door and into
the forest. Never again did she go
wandering in the forest near the home
of the three bears.

THE SNOW QUEEN

Saviour Pirotta
Illustrated by Lucy Fleming

Once upon a time, a long, long time ago, an evil snow queen owned a horrible mirror. Everything reflected in it, no matter how beautiful, looked hideous.

But one day, the mirror broke and
it shattered into a million fragments.

The wind scattered the fragments
to all corners of the world.
A tiny sliver of glass fell
into a window box
full of roses.

It lay there, hidden,
until one summer...

"Ouch," said Kai, who was
watering the roses with his
best friend Gerda. "There's
something in my eye."

The glass instantly froze Kai's heart. Everything he saw now looked nasty and horrible.

In a rage, he tore the roses to shreds. Gerda, who loved all living things, was heartbroken.

Winter came and Kai was still angry with the world. One day, while he was out riding on his sled, he saw a sleigh.

He was tired, so he decided to hitch his sled to it.

He did not know that it was the Snow Queen's sleigh.
"Sit beside me," she said, smiling a cool smile.
And with that, Kai was under her spell.

The Snow Queen's sleigh swooped up high into the sky,
carrying Kai far from home.

Spring was approaching and Kai had still not returned home. Gerda set out to find him.

"He was kidnapped by the Snow Queen," chirped Gerda's friend, the river bird.

"I shall find a boat and
sail to the Snow Queen's
palace," said Gerda.

Soon Gerda came to a summer
island where a witch lived.

"Why don't you stay?"
said the witch, offering
Gerda a cherry.

One bite of the ripe fruit, and Gerda forgot all about Kai.

But later, she woke up from the spell and remembered.

She returned to her boat and set off again to find Kai.

Away she sailed, up rivers and far across seas, getting colder and colder until the boat got stuck in the ice.

"How shall I get to the Snow Queen's palace now?" exclaimed Gerda loudly.

"You can borrow Bae, my reindeer," said a girl who was fishing nearby.

Bae carried Gerda to the Snow
Queen's palace. The Snow Queen was
away but she had left Kai behind.

"I've come to
take you home,"
cried Gerda.

Kai looked puzzled.
He did not recognize Gerda.

Saddened, Gerda kissed him and her
tears warmed Kai's heart. The sliver
of mirror fell from his eye.

"Gerda? Is it you?" Kai exclaimed. "Where are we?"
Gerda's tears turned to joy at Kai's words.

"We are in great danger," she said.

"Let's go home before the Snow Queen returns."

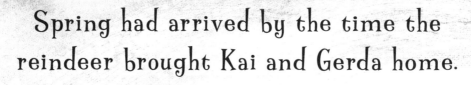

Spring had arrived by the time the
reindeer brought Kai and Gerda home.

150

New roses bloomed in the window box. Kai thought they were the most precious things in the world.

HANSEL AND GRETEL

Amanda Askew

Illustrated by Bruno Merz

153

Once upon a time, Hansel and Gretel lived
in a tiny cottage with their father, a poor
woodcutter, and their cruel stepmother.

"There are too many mouths to feed,"
their stepmother told the woodcutter.
"Take the children miles from home, so far
that they can never find their way back!"

Overhearing the conversation, Hansel slipped
out of the house, filled his pockets with
pebbles, and then went back to bed.

All night long, the woodcutter's wife nagged her husband. The next day, he led Hansel and Gretel away into the forest.

As they walked through
the trees, Hansel dropped the
pebbles here and there.

Suddenly, the woodcutter slipped away and
the children found themselves alone.
Gretel began to sob bitterly.

"Don't cry," said Hansel. "I'll take you home,
even if Father doesn't come back for us!"

Luckily, the moon was full that night, and
the pebbles gleamed in the moonlight.

The children found their way home
and crept through a half-open window
without waking their parents.

When their stepmother discovered that Hansel
and Gretel had returned, she was angry.

She kept Hansel and Gretel under lock and key all
day, with only a sip of water and some stale bread.

When dawn came, the woodcutter led the
children out into the forest once again.

Hansel, however, had not eaten his bread,
and as he walked through the trees, he left
a trail of crumbs to mark the way.

Again the children found themselves alone.

"Don't worry. I've left a trail, like last time," Hansel whispered to Gretel.

Sadly, the little boy had forgotten about the hungry animals in the forest. In no time at all, the crumbs had all been eaten.

When dawn broke, they wandered
through the forest. On and on they walked,
till they came upon a strange cottage.

"This is chocolate!" gasped Hansel as he broke a lump of plaster from the wall.

"And this is icing!" exclaimed Gretel, putting a bit of a doorpost in her mouth.

Starving but delighted, the children began to eat pieces of the cottage.

Quietly, the cookie door swung open.
There stood an old woman.

"Well, well," said the old woman, peering at them. "You children have quite a sweet tooth! Come in and eat what you wish."

Unluckily for Hansel and Gretel, the delicious cottage belonged to a witch. They had fallen into her trap.

"You're nothing but skin and bones," cried the witch, locking Hansel into a cage. "I shall fatten you up and eat you!"

"You will do the housework," she told Gretel. "Then I'll make a meal of you, too!"

Each day, the witch would feel Hansel's finger.
The witch had poor eyesight, so he held out a chicken bone.

"Too thin!" she complained.
"When will you become plump?"

At last the witch grew tired of waiting...

"Light the oven," she told Gretel. "We're going to have roasted boy today!"

When the witch bent down to see if the oven
was hot enough, Gretel gave her a tremendous
push and slammed the oven door shut.

Free at last, the children stayed at the cottage, eating candy. After a few days, they found a huge chocolate egg filled with gold coins.

"The witch is burned to a cinder now," said Hansel. "We'll take the treasure home with us, to Father."

They set off into the forest, and on the second day, they found their way home. Their wicked stepmother left in disgust, so Hansel, Gretel, and their father lived happily ever after.

Next Steps

Show the children the opening page of each story. Do they know what the story is about just by looking at that page and the title?

There are lots of different characters in this book. Some are good and some are bad! Explain that words we use to describe are called adjectives. Try playing the following game. Ask the children to think of a main character and use three adjectives that best describe them. The rest of the group should then guess which character is being described.

Ask the children who the main characters are in each story. How do we know they are the main characters? Ask the children to draw their favorite character from the book.

Ask the children what each story made them think about. When were the characters sad? When were they scared? They could choose their favorite part from each story and act out the scene, using facial expressions to show the characters' emotions.

What alternative endings for each story can the children think of? Ask them to pick one story from the book and write a new ending.